This book is for

_____

With love from

_____

On

_____

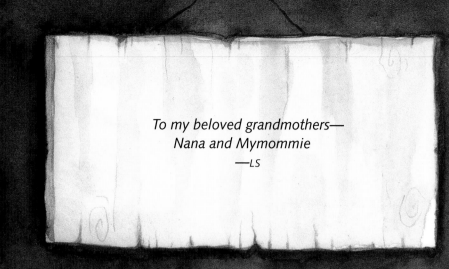

To my beloved grandmothers—
Nana and Mymommie
—LS

ZONDERKIDZ

Love is Kind
Copyright © 2018 by Laura Sassi
Illustrations © 2018 by Lison Chaperon

This title is also available as a Zondervan ebook.

Requests for information should be addressed to:
Zonderkidz, 3900 Sparks Dr., Grand Rapids, Michigan 49546

ISBN 978-0-310-75489-3

Scripture quotations marked NIrV are taken from the Holy Bible, New International Reader's Version®, NIrV®. Copyright © 1995, 1996, 1998, 2014 by Biblica, Inc.® Used by permission of Zondervan. All rights reserved worldwide. www.zondervan.com. The "NIrV" and "New International Reader's Version" are trademarks registered in the United States Patent and Trademark Office by Biblica, Inc.®

Any Internet addresses (websites, blogs, etc.) and telephone numbers in this book are offered as a resource. They are not intended in any way to be or imply an endorsement by Zondervan, nor does Zondervan vouch for the content of these sites and numbers for the life of this book.

Art direction and design: Jody Langley

Printed in the USA

18 19 20 21 22 23 /PC/ 22 21 20 19 18 17 16 15 14 13 12 11 10 9 8 7 6 5 4 3 2

Love is Kind

Written by
Laura Sassi

Illustrated by
Lison Chaperon

ZONDERkidz

Little Owl jingled the coins in his pocket. It was Grammy's birthday. And, finally, he had enough money to buy her something special—a heart-shaped box of chocolates.

He took out the coins—so shiny and new—and ready to spend. But then …

"Oh no! Come back!"
The coins rolled down until **wobble PING**
they landed right by Beaver's dam.

Beaver cheered. "Mommy, you were wrong! The tooth fairy came after all. She brought me THREE silver coins!"

"Wait!" Little Owl hollered, "Those are mi …"

But then he stopped. Beaver looked so happy.
"Wow, you're lucky. Have a tooth-errific day!"
said Little Owl.

His gift for Grammy would have to wait.

As he headed back home, something caught Little Owl's eye. Money! "I can buy that heart-shaped box of chocolates after all!"

That's when he saw the sign.

MISSING
$ 1.00
if found return to
Mrs. Mouse

Little Owl's feathers quivered. He really
wanted those chocolates for Grammy.
But he did not want to buy them with
Mrs. Mouse's money.

Ding-dong. "I think this is yours."

Mrs. Mouse clapped her paws. "Thank you! Now I can get the nursery ready. Mr. Mouse and I are expecting babies!"

Little Owl smiled. "That's wonderful news. Congratulations!"

Little Owl shuffled on. Then ...

THUMP!

He bumped into Rabbit.

Rabbit had THREE heart-shaped boxes of chocolates.

"For Ma,

for Pa,

and for ME!" Rabbit sang.

Little Owl's feathers stood on end.
"You have THREE! That's not fai ..."

Little Owl stopped.
Getting angry wouldn't get
Grammy those chocolates.

Little Owl took a deep breath.

"That's nice, Rabbit. Enjoy your candy."

"Thanks," said Rabbit. Then off she hopped.

Love does not envy...

It is not easily angered...

It does not dishonor others.

Little Owl's heart felt empty. So much for getting
Grammy something special.

But then …

Rabbit hopped back and handed Little Owl a coupon. "So you can get some too." "Good for one box of Chipmunk's Famous Chocolates!"

Little Owl flipped. "I'm getting Grammy chocolates! I'm getting Grammy chocolates!"

Love is not self-seeking...
It always hopes.

He danced through the meadow to
Chipmunk's Chocolate Shoppe.

HATS

Closed

ORGANIC
CHOCOLATE
SHOPPE

CLOSED

But just as he rounded
the corner, he spotted
Chipmunk holding a sign
that said, "Closed."

Little Owl gasped. "Are you closing for the day?"

"Sure am," Chipmunk chattered. "I need to make more chocolates for the morning."

Little Owl gulped. "I understand. Have a good night."

Little Owl had nothing to give
Grammy for her birthday.
Nothing, but a crinkled coupon.

Then—**whoosh**—the wind snatched even that away.

Empty-winged,
Little Owl slumped
all the way to Grammy's.

"Why so glum?"
Grammy asked.

Little Owl tried to hold back the tears. Then he told Grammy
all about Beaver and Mrs. Mouse and Rabbit and Chipmunk's
Chocolate Shoppe.

Grammy smiled. "Little Owl, you spread love everywhere you went today. That's better than any heart-shaped box of chocolates!"

Little Owl's feather's twitched. "Really?"

Love never gives up.
Love never fails.

He looked at his reflection in Grammy's picture window and giggled.
"Well, it's not chocolate, but I guess I did give you a heart-shaped gift after all!"

ME!

"And that is the best gift of all," said Grammy.